# I Want to Go to the Fair!

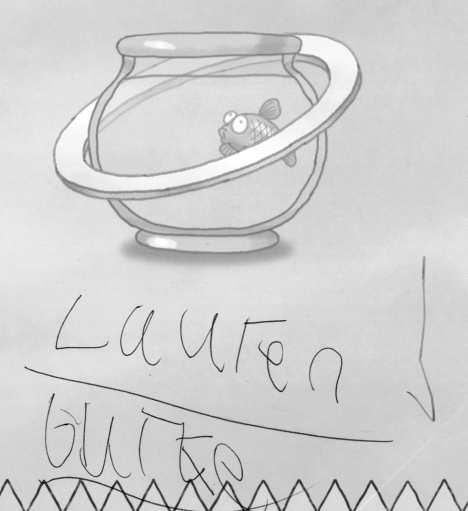

Lauren
Guite

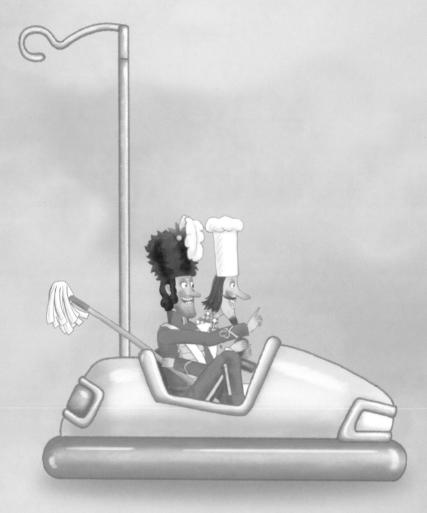

Licensed by The Illuminated Film Company
Based on the LITTLE PRINCESS animation series © The Illuminated Film Company 2008
Made under licence by Andersen Press Ltd., London
'I Want to Go to the Fair!' episode written by Kelly Marshall.
Producer Iain Harvey.  Director Edward Foster.
© The Illuminated Film Company/Tony Ross 2008
Design and layout © Andersen Press Ltd, 2008.
Printed and bound in China by C&C Offset Printing.
10   9   8   7   6   5   4   3   2   1
British Library Cataloguing in Publication Data available.

ISBN: 978 1 84270 763 0 (Trade edition)
ISBN: 978 1 84939 693 6 (Riverside Books edition)

# I Want to Go to the Fair!

**Tony Ross**

Andersen Press · London

The Little Princess picked up a bouncy ball and threw it at the
row of toys lined up on the window ledge. "I'm practising for
the fair! It's almost time to go."

**Boinng!!** Humpty Dumpty was sent flying.
"I'm going to go on a bouncy castle and bumper cars," giggled the
Little Princess, "and I'm going to win a big orange goldfish!"
It was very exciting.

"Is everybody here?" called the King.
The castle hall was crammed with people, itching to get
to the fair.
"I'm here!" chimed the Little Princess.

She couldn't resist hopping down the stairs two at a time, and doing a little twirl at the bottom.

The Queen rounded everyone up. "Right-ho, off to the fair we go!"

The Little Princess made a dash for the door. "I'm a bumper car!

# Beep, beep!"

"Careful, Princess," warned the Prime Minister. "Mind you
don't trip."

But it was too late.

**Crash!** The Little Princess tumbled over the General's hobbyhorse.

The King and Queen hurried over. "Are you OK, dear?"

"My foot hurts!" cried the Little Princess.

"Sorry, Princess. No fair for you," said the Doctor, as she wrapped the Little Princess's leg in a tight bandage.

The Little Princess tried to get up. "No! Look, I can still…oww!"

"Careful, poppet," frowned the King.

"You heard the Doctor," sighed the Queen. "You'll have to stay at home today." The Little Princess howled. "But I want to go to the fair!"

The Little Princess felt very sad watching the others getting ready.

"Have we got everything?" asked the Maid.
The King whispered loudly in the Queen's ear. "Maybe we should all stay at home?"
The crowd hushed at once, then turned to the Queen.
"Don't be silly," she answered. "We're going to have lots of fun, aren't we, Princess?"
The Little Princess frowned. "No!"

"Ta-da!" The Chef held up a bag of delicious cakes. "Nibbles for the journey."
The Little Princess looked even more fed up.

"Off you go," shooed the Queen. "Have a good time!"

"Chin up, sailor!" smiled the Admiral, as everyone trooped out.

The Queen put her hands on her hips. "Right then! Plenty of fun coming up."

"It won't be as good as the fair," groaned the Little Princess.

The Queen squeezed the Little Princess into a trolley packed with things.

"We're going to have our own little fair," she explained. "How does that sound?" The Little Princess sighed. "Horrible."

But the Queen wasn't going to give up that easily.

On the other side of the kingdom, the royal
household arrived at the fair.
"Come on then, everyone!" marshalled the
King. "Keep together."

"Let's start with trolley racing!" cried
the Queen.
The Little Princess was not impressed.
"OK," said her mum. "Have a go
on your very own pineapple shy!"
"Throwing balls is boring,"
grumbled the
Little Princess.

The Queen stopped. "So you don't want to play any of these games?"

"N-O."

"Well, all right," said her mum. "But that means the only thing left is bedtime."

The Little Princess crossed her arms and sulked. She wasn't
even tired.

"Here we are," said the Queen. "Bedtime."

The Little Princess blinked. "Huh? This isn't my bed."

"No, it's mine," announced her mum. "Much better to bounce on." The Queen patted the mattress and grinned, but the Little Princess looked away.

"If that's how you want it to be," sighed the Queen, "I'll just have to show you."

"Stop!" cried the Little Princess. "I don't want to…ooh!"
The bed was getting bouncier and bouncier.
"Do you want to go higher?" asked the Queen.

The Little Princess couldn't resist any longer. "Yes! Higher, higher!"

The Queen jumped up to the ceiling, then landed with a CRASH! onto the carpet. The Little Princess gasped, until she heard her mum shriek with laughter.

While the royal household bumped on the dodgems, the Little Princess was having some fun of her own.

# "Out of the way, Puss!"

squealed the Little Princess. "I'm a bumper car!"
The Queen became redder and redder, but her
plan was working. The Little Princess was
actually starting to enjoy herself.

Over at the fairground, the King finally managed to
toss a hoopla onto a goldfish.
Back at the castle, the Little Princess's hoopla landed
straight on the Queen's nose.
"W-well done, dear," stuttered the Queen.

While the Admiral tried to hook a duckie, the Little Princess
caught a prize of her own.
"Ooh! A goldfish!" she beamed. The Queen wiped the pondweed
off her frock and smiled wearily.

It was the end of a lovely day.

"I wish the Princess was here," sighed the Chef.

The Gardener nodded. "She would have really liked it."

"Poor Princess," agreed the King. "She missed all the fun. I hope this goldfish will make her feel better." "Castle off the starboard bow!" cried the Admiral, pointing towards home.

"Poppet, we're home!" boomed the King. "And look what we've won for you."

"Sshh!" whispered the Little Princess. "You'll wake Mummy."

The Queen sat quietly in her chair, fast asleep.
The Little Princess pointed at the bowl next to her bed.
"I won him at my fair."
"But what shall I do with *this* goldfish?" asked the King.

The Little Princess thought for a moment and then giggled…

"Now Mummy can have one too!"